P9-CDI-338

This book belongs to ...

____

THE CAT
IN
THE
HAT
By
Dr. Seuss
RANDOM
HOUSE

Special thanks to the University of California, San Diego, Geisel Library, Mandeville Special Collections Department for providing material from the Seuss Collection.

This title was originally catalogued by the Library of Congress as follows: Seuss, Dr. The cat in the hat, by Dr. Seuss [pseud.] Boston, Houghton Mifflin [1957] 61 p. illus. 24 cm. I. Title. PZ8.3.G276Cat 56-5470 ISBN 0-394-80001-X ISBN 0-394-90001-4.

The sun did not shine.
It was too wet to play.
So we sat in the house
All that cold, cold, wet day.

I sat there with Sally.
We sat there, we two.
And I said, "How I wish
We had something to do!"

Too wet to go out
And too cold to play ball.
So we sat in the house.
We did nothing at all.

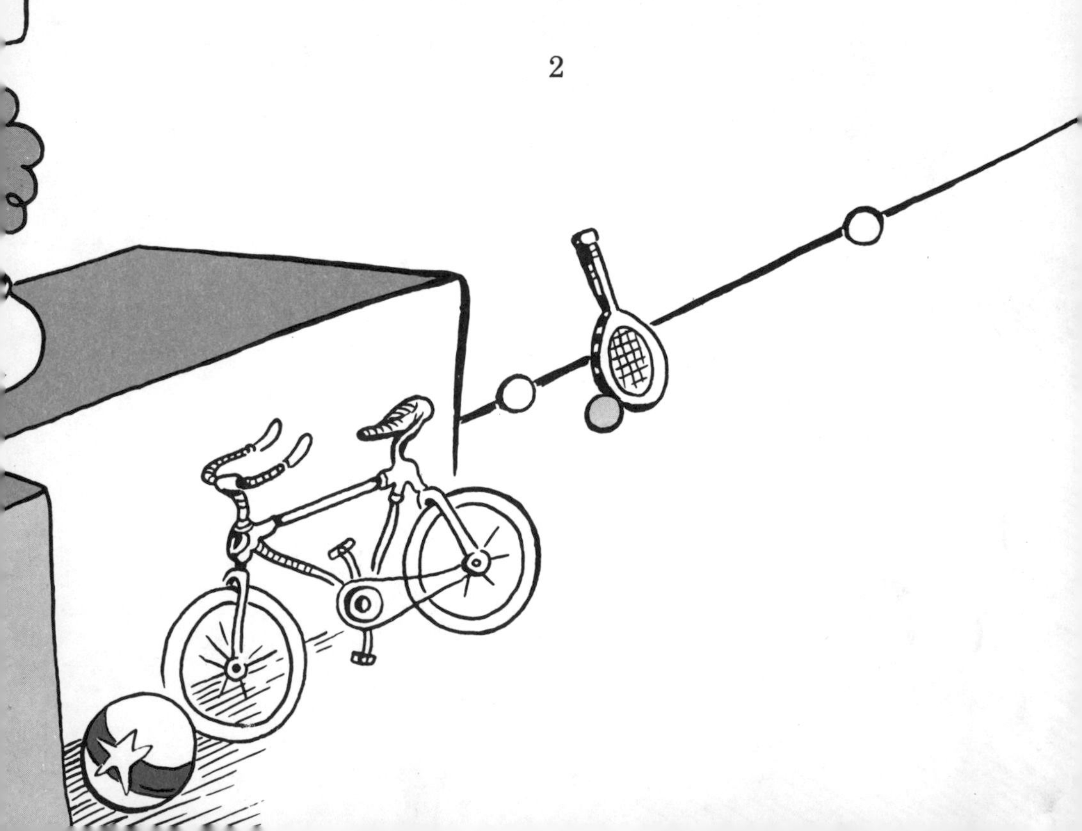

So all we could do was to

Sit!

Sit!

Sit!

Sit!

And we did not like it.

Not one little bit.

And then

Something went BUMP!

How that bump made us jump!

We looked!

Then we saw him step in on the mat!

We looked!

And we saw him!

The Cat in the Hat!

And he said to us,

"Why do you sit there like that?"

"I know it is wet
And the sun is not sunny.
But we can have
Lots of good fun that is funny!"

"I know some good games we could play,"
Said the cat.
"I know some new tricks,"
Said the Cat in the Hat.
"A lot of good tricks.
I will show them to you.
Your mother
Will not mind at all if I do."

Then Sally and I
Did not know what to say.
Our mother was out of the house
For the day.

But our fish said, "No! No!
Make that cat go away!
Tell that Cat in the Hat
You do NOT want to play.
He should not be here.
He should not be about.
He should not be here
When your mother is out!"

"Now! Now! Have no fear.
Have no fear!" said the cat.
"My tricks are not bad,"
Said the Cat in the Hat.
"Why, we can have
Lots of good fun, if you wish,
With a game that I call
UP-UP-UP with a fish!"

"Put me down!" said the fish.
"This is no fun at all!
Put me down!" said the fish.
"I do NOT wish to fall!"

"Have no fear!" said the cat.
"I will not let you fall.
I will hold you up high
As I stand on a ball.
With a book on one hand!
And a cup on my hat!
But that is not ALL I can do!"
Said the cat . . .

"Look at me!

Look at me now!" said the cat.

"With a cup and a cake

On the top of my hat!

I can hold up TWO books!

I can hold up the fish!

And a little toy ship!

And some milk on a dish!

And look!

I can hop up and down on the ball!

But that is not all!

Oh, no.

That is not all . . .

"Look at me!
Look at me!
Look at me NOW!
It is fun to have fun
But you have to know how.
I can hold up the cup
And the milk and the cake!
I can hold up these books!
And the fish on a rake!
I can hold the toy ship
And a little toy man!
And look! With my tail
I can hold a red fan!
I can fan with the fan
As I hop on the ball!
But that is not all.
Oh, no.
That is not all. . . ."

That is what the cat said . . .
Then he fell on his head!
He came down with a bump
From up there on the ball.
And Sally and I,
We saw ALL the things fall!

And our fish came down, too.

He fell into a pot!

He said, “Do I like this?

Oh, no! I do not.

This is not a good game,”

Said our fish as he lit.

“No, I do not like it,

Not one little bit!”

"Now look what you did!"
Said the fish to the cat.
"Now look at this house!
Look at this! Look at that!
You sank our toy ship,
Sank it deep in the cake.
You shook up our house
And you bent our new rake.
You SHOULD NOT be here
When our mother is not.
You get out of this house!"
Said the fish in the pot.

"But I like to be here.
Oh, I like it a lot!"
Said the Cat in the Hat
To the fish in the pot.
"I will NOT go away.
I do NOT wish to go!
And so," said the Cat in the Hat,
"So

so

so . . .
I will show you
Another good game that I know!"

And then he ran out.

And, then, fast as a fox,

The Cat in the Hat

Came back in with a box.

A big red wood box.

It was shut with a hook.

"Now look at this trick,"

Said the cat.

"Take a look!"

Then he got up on top
With a tip of his hat.
"I call this game FUN-IN-A-BOX,"
Said the cat.
"In this box are two things
I will show to you now.
You will like these two things,"
Said the cat with a bow.

"I will pick up the hook.
You will see something new.
Two things. And I call them
Thing One and Thing Two.
These Things will not bite you.
They want to have fun."
Then, out of the box
Came Thing Two and Thing One!
And they ran to us fast.
They said, "How do you do?
Would you like to shake hands
With Thing One and Thing Two?"

And Sally and I
Did not know what to do.
So we had to shake hands
With Thing One and Thing Two.
We shook their two hands.
But our fish said, "No! No!
Those Things should not be
In this house! Make them go!

“They should not be here
When your mother is not!
Put them out! Put them out!”
Said the fish in the pot.

"Have no fear, little fish,"
Said the Cat in the Hat.
"These Things are good Things."
And he gave them a pat.
"They are tame. Oh, so tame!
They have come here to play.
They will give you some fun
On this wet, wet, wet day."

"Now, here is a game that they like,"

Said the cat.

"They like to fly kites,"

Said the Cat in the Hat.

"No! Not in the house!"
Said the fish in the pot.
"They should not fly kites
In a house! They should not.
Oh, the things they will bump!
Oh, the things they will hit!
Oh, I do not like it!
Not one little bit!"

Then Sally and I
Saw them run down the hall.
We saw those two Things
Bump their kites on the wall!
Bump! Thump! Thump! Bump!
Down the wall in the hall.

THIN
1

Thing Two and Thing One!
They ran up! They ran down!
On the string of one kite
We saw Mother's new gown!
Her gown with the dots
That are pink, white and red.
Then we saw one kite bump
On the head of her bed!

Then those Things ran about
With big bumps, jumps and kicks
And with hops and big thumps
And all kinds of bad tricks.
And I said,
"I do NOT like the way that they play!
If Mother could see this,
Oh, what would she say!"

Then our fish said, "Look! Look!"
And our fish shook with fear.
"Your mother is on her way home!
Do you hear?
Oh, what will she do to us?
What will she say?
Oh, she will not like it
To find us this way!"

"So, DO something! Fast!" said the fish.
"Do you hear!
I saw her. Your mother!
Your mother is near!
So, as fast as you can,
Think of something to do!
You will have to get rid of
Thing One and Thing Two!"

So, as fast as I could,
I went after my net.
And I said, "With my net
I can get them I bet.
I bet, with my net,
I can get those Things yet!"

Then I let down my net.
It came down with a PLOP!
And I had them! At last!
Those two Things had to stop.
Then I said to the cat,
"Now you do as I say.
You pack up those Things
And you take them away!"

"Oh dear!" said the cat.

"You did not like our game . . .

Oh dear.

What a shame!

What a shame!

What a shame!"

Then he shut up the Things
In the box with the hook.
And the cat went away
With a sad kind of look.

"That is good," said the fish.
"He has gone away. Yes.
But your mother will come.
She will find this big mess!
And this mess is so big
And so deep and so tall,
We can not pick it up.
There is no way at all!"

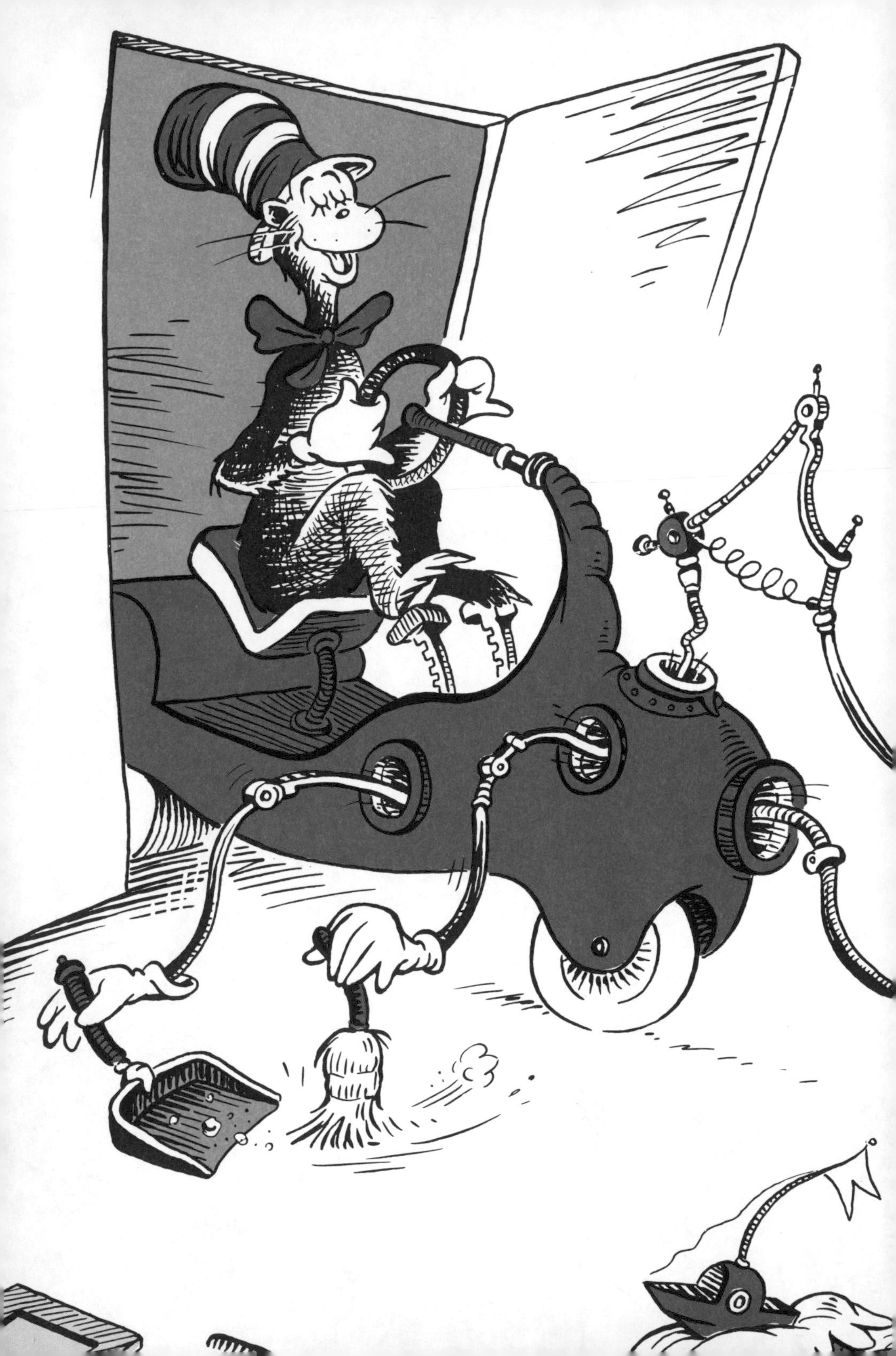

And THEN!

Who was back in the house?

Why, the cat!

"Have no fear of this mess,"

Said the Cat in the Hat.

"I always pick up all my playthings

And so . . .

I will show you another

Good trick that I know!"

Then we saw him pick up
All the things that were down.
He picked up the cake,
And the rake, and the gown,
And the milk, and the strings,
And the books, and the dish,
And the fan, and the cup,
And the ship, and the fish.
And he put them away.
Then he said, "That is that."
And then he was gone
With a tip of his hat.

Then our mother came in
And she said to us two,
"Did you have any fun?
Tell me. What did you do?"

And Sally and I did not know
What to say.
Should we tell her
The things that went on there that day?

Should we tell her about it?

Now, what SHOULD we do?

Well . . .

What would YOU do

If your mother asked YOU?

SPECIAL EDITION
CELEBRATING THE
40th
BIRTHDAY of
THE CAT IN THE HAT

HAPPY 40th BIRTHDAY, CAT IN THE HAT

UPI/Corbis-Bettmann

Dr. Seuss brought the Cat in the Hat to life forty years ago. Now children and adults everywhere know the fun-loving cat in the red-and-white hat. But who was Dr. Seuss?

Dr. Seuss's real name was Theodor Seuss Geisel, but everyone called him Ted. As a boy growing up in Springfield, Massachusetts, Ted loved to read, draw, and make up silly stories. He drew cartoons and wrote stories all through school.

At Dartmouth College Ted began signing his cartoons with his middle name, *Seuss*. He added the title *Doctor* later. Soon Ted was known simply as Dr. Seuss.

In 1937 Dr. Seuss wrote and illustrated a children's book called *And to Think That I Saw It on Mulberry Street.*

AP/Wide World Photos

Above: Dr. Seuss reads to 4-year-old Lucinda Bell at his home in 1956.
Below: Something almost seen on Mulberry Street.

Although it was rejected twenty-eight times before it was finally published, children loved the book, and it became a huge success. Many wonderful storybooks followed.

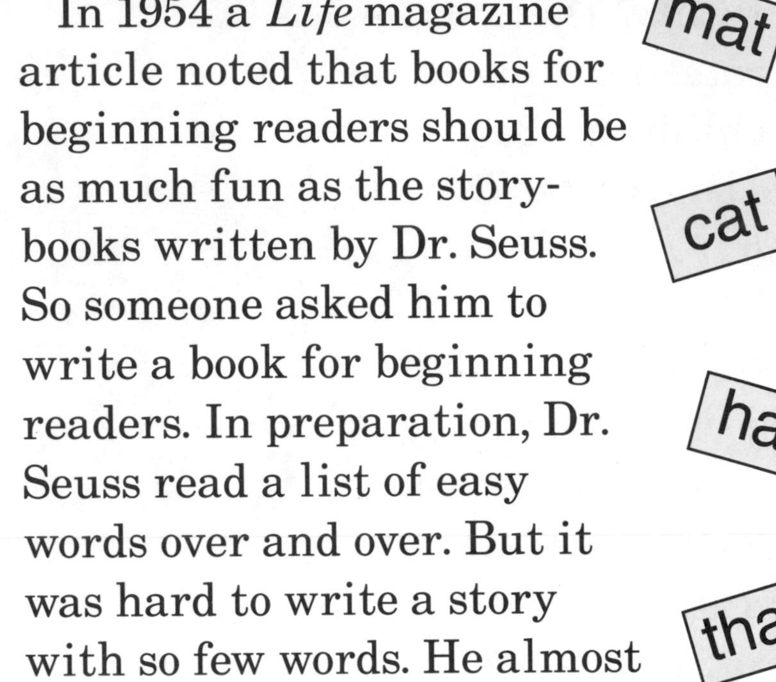

In 1954 a *Life* magazine article noted that books for beginning readers should be as much fun as the storybooks written by Dr. Seuss. So someone asked him to write a book for beginning readers. In preparation, Dr. Seuss read a list of easy words over and over. But it was hard to write a story with so few words. He almost gave up.

"Look at me!
Look at me now!" said the cat.
"With a cup and a cake
On the top of my hat!
I can hold up TWO books!
I can hold up the fish!
And a little toy ship!
And some milk on a dish!
And look!
I can hop up and down on the ball!
But that is not all!
Oh, no.
That is not all . . .

16

Then he read the list one more time. The first two words that rhymed became his title: *The Cat in the Hat*. Dr. Seuss drew a cat with a tall, striped hat. Suddenly the story started to fall into place!

But it was not easy. "Writing books for kids is hard work, a lot harder than most people realize," Dr. Seuss observed.

Above: Pencil and ink from *The Cat in the Hat Comes Back*. Opposite and below: Finished pages and working rough drawing for *The Cat in the Hat*.

Courtesy Mandeville Special Collections Library, University of California, San Diego.

It took him over a year to write and draw the story of *The Cat in the Hat*. And what a story it was: the cat was full of mischief! Kids couldn't wait to turn the pages to find out what happened. *The Cat in the Hat* was easy to read, but, more important, it made learning to read fun.

Greta Pratt/Reuters/Archive Photos

The Cat in the Hat flies high in the Macy's Thanksgiving Day Parade.

Burt Steel/AP/Wide World Photos

Dr. Seuss shakes hands with a good friend.

Ken Levine/AP/Wide World Photos

Cats seemed to follow him wherever he went.

This groundbreaking book was published in 1957. It was so successful that it launched a new career for Dr. Seuss, as president and editor in chief of Beginner Books. This new division of Random House was created to develop fun, easy-to-read books for children. The cat became its symbol, and Dr. Seuss often said that cats seemed to follow him everywhere for the rest of his life.

Theodor Seuss Geisel 1904–1991
Portrait of Theodor Seuss Geisel, Class of 1925, by Everett Raymond Kinstler, 1982.
Commissioned by the Trustees of Dartmouth College, Hanover, N.H.

Over his lifetime Dr. Seuss never stopped doing what he loved to do most: writing, drawing, and having fun! His books are still favorites of children and their parents everywhere, and his stories will continue to delight readers for years to come.

Then he said, "That is that."
And then he was gone
With a tip of his hat.